My Brother's Basement

Stories and Interludes

Joy Huebert

Quadra Books

Library and Archives Canada Cataloguing in Publication

Huebert, Joy Louise, author
My brother's basement : stories and interludes / Joy Louise Huebert.

ISBN 978-0-9939223-3-6 (paperback)

I. Title.

PS8615.U313M9 2016   C813'.6   C2016-903767-3

Published by Quadra Books
Victoria, BC, Canada
www.quadrabooks.com

This book is dedicated to
Harold, Jack,
Dave and Don

My Brother's Basement
Stories and Interludes

My Brother's Basement

Our family basement was embedded in the earth, lined with cracked concrete, the dark ceiling mysteriously an underneath of the kitchen floor above. Cobwebs, a potato storage bin, and shelves with junk lined the dark unpleasant space. In winter, I scraped frost off the walls with my fingernails, amazed at how the outside could come in. Two small windows high up did little to penetrate the gloom. A huge furnace lurked in one corner, the cause of much concern. Acquired at great expense, the furnace replaced an oil burner that still sat against one wall. My parents would study it and discuss whether it would eventually blow up and kill us all.

My mother spent a lot of time down there doing laundry. She owned a wringer-washer that churned clothes in hot soapy water. After the churning stopped, she would pull the sodden garments through a wringer while telling stories of how a careless woman's arm had been caught up in the rollers and crushed. Like the furnace, the washer was a fearsome thing. My mother would hang the clothes on lines outside in summer, or on lines in the basement in winter. With three children, she spent many hours every week doing this chore. One day she showed us our grandmother's washboard. In that process, clothes were immersed in a wooden tub and then scrubbed up against the glass washboard ridges. The woman became the churn. No doubt my grandmother felt more fortunate than women of the past with flat rocks and a river. It was a relief when more money allowed my parents to purchase an automatic washer and dryer.

The throngs of children in my extended family would be sent to the basement so that our raucous play would not disturb the grownups upstairs.

Now, after a period of upstairs adulthood, I have taken up basement dwelling. It happened like this: after high school I went to work at the Great Waste of Life, AKA Great West Life Insurance Company. It was to be a short sojourn to save money and then travel to Europe before enjoying a university education. Unfortunately, I met the other Great Waste of Life, my husband Gerald, a struggling musician who needed a lot of support, both emotionally and financially. I was captivated by his dark curly hair, dark eyes, charming singing voice and what turned out to be a major drinking problem. I have written many drafts of a novel about all this, but have moved on. I encourage you to enter a search in the public library catalogue using the terms "spouse with a drinking problem" and you will get the story from those who are better storytellers. I assure you, after the first flurry of exciting romance, and the next flurries of regret, fighting, hitting bottom and then reuniting based on lies of change and love, it's all quite boring. You will thank me for keeping this part of the story brief. In short, I decided to throw my dull secure job away, part finally from the singing man, and move into my only option, my brother's basement. (SEE: "Home is where if you go there, they have to take you in." Thanks, My Brother.)

Frankly, I suspect that Don was thinking of my habitation as a temporary sojourn. I may have given him to believe I just wanted respite while seeking another apartment, but I have come to appreciate basement living and mean to stay.

Don's house was built in 1950, with beautiful plaster walls, coved ceilings and hardwood floors. The kitchen hasn't been changed, as cooking is not one of my brother's interests. The worn original linoleum is not a feature, simply something underfoot to walk on. His basement, on the other hand, was renovated in the 1970s with cheap plywood covering cement walls, and a bathroom thrown into a corner. Slightly newer linoleum covers the concrete floor, and the small barred windows set high in the walls on the east and west of the long narrow room let in a little light. Here it is I live my artist life, a washed-up insurance clerk endeavouring to write fiction and wrestle creative substance from a barely furnished space provided rent-free by a brother whose good job allows me the charity of family. The room is furnished with a couch and chair rescued from my grandparents' basement upon their move to a seniors facility. Who knows from which basement they had acquired the floral furniture with a weave that evokes hemp bags filled with potatoes. I sleep in a narrow bed that accommodates one person - a person with a realistic awareness that this bed will be fine, will likely never need to include someone else. That part of my life is over, now to be turned into fiction. I feel I have a story to tell, one that includes a plot, characters, and plenty of revenge.

It never occurred to me that I would not be able to write a novel. Story lines have been cramming my head for as long as I've been alive, but I've always been too busy mulling over life insurance policies, and propping up my husband, to pay them much attention. Now that I have all the time in the world, I've been struggling. Here is my day: I wake up but don't go upstairs until my brother leaves for work. He's been a little testy lately about my contribution to the groceries and cooking. My mother used to do all the shopping and prepare meals for him, but I'm not into that. I need my time and attention for my novel. When he leaves I go upstairs and eat some cereal. Then I have a cup of coffee and listen to the CBC news. It's important to stay informed. I can't help but go to my iPad, where I play Scrabble on Facebook. I am currently playing twenty games at a time. These games sharpen the language skills that I need for writing. At some point, maybe midmorning, a sentence arises in me. Often it is a perfect sentence, but so far, not connected to a paragraph or a story. Nevertheless I feel very hopeful. I write this sentence down and think about it. Is it in the best verb tense? Are the adjectives stale or cliched? Can I strengthen the imagery? Or, horrors, is there an adverb? I tinker with the sentence and then feel tired and go lie down for awhile. Then it is time for lunch. My brother has taken to eating at his work cafeteria, so lunch can be a repeat of breakfast, there being no groceries.

The early afternoon is a good time to relate to soap operas or watch television shows that I have recorded, such as *The Daily Show* or *The Big Bang Theory*. Popular culture can be food for the creative life. The late afternoon is a good time for a long bath. I think about going for a walk, but leave it in case another sentence comes to me. It's all good. It's all so good.

One morning my brother called down to me and said a man was coming to power-wash the house to prepare it for painting. He asked me to give him the cheque that was lying on the table. I agreed. He went on to say that sometimes people did their own power-washing, but he was too busy with his job. He said that even women can power-wash.

During breakfast I began to fantasize about the man coming to clean the house. Would this be a good premise for a novel? The plot could evolve as a romance of the sort that seemed to be selling well. He could have beautiful blue eyes, and a muscular body rippling under a tight t-shirt. Louise could go outside to give him a cheque, their eyes could meet and they could banter. The rest of the plot would write itself. I went back downstairs to mull over a perfect sentence. Eventually I could hear the loud noise of a house being sprayed with water jets. I got up and went outside.

"Hello." I called out to a man on a high ladder holding a heavy machine.

I noticed he was approximately seventeen years old, with many tattoos. I am thirty-seven, and don't feel like writing that kind of novel.

He didn't hear me, so I went back inside. If all I could imagine for a novel premise was a romance involving power-washing, I needed more creative fodder. I'd already decided that my life with a drunken musician was too boring to write down, but I'd been in my brother's basement for three weeks now, and had nothing but a handful of perfect sentences, leading nowhere. Here is an example: The living and the dead got together to write family stories, and those who were listening couldn't tell them apart.

One problem was that my mother had been living in the basement. Obviously it wasn't big enough for the two of us, so I talked her into moving to the guest room of my other brother in Vancouver. With a better climate and a lovely daughter-in-law who prepares delicious meals, she has come to feel very much at home. My Vancouver brother has taken to phoning me and asking when I might be moving on, but with call display I have been able to avoid these calls. I'm really happy with things as they are and my mother with her sore knees is better off in a guest room than a basement. My brother's marriage is a little complacent, so the stress of looking after an aging parent should give it some much needed shaking up.

That's how I came to be in the basement. Once I finish my novel and sell it for lots of money, everyone will be happy.

Storylines

Dear Dave,

After hearing so much about you, I sure was happy to finally meet in person at the writer's conference. Your workshop on street names in the modern Canadian urban literary landscape was inspiring, and I thought you might like my story, *The Waterfall* (attached). It is about a woman driven mad while on vacation with her family. She longs to push her husband over a huge waterfall, but instead becomes ill, lies in bed and fantasizes about a giant bronze statue called Portlandia. It's a very sensitive story about a woman's journey. There are no street names in the story, but if you could suggest some, I would be deeply grateful.

Any comments you may have would be helpful.

Love,

Louise

P. S. I will never forget that night by the ocean when we kicked off our shoes and you kissed my toes. Is there any chance you might be heading out this way some time?

Dear Louise:

Readable art therapy.

Stylistically, it comes across to me like *The Ballad of Lucy Jordan* written by a sober Charles Bukowski; it is equal parts simple sentences, repetition, and quiet desperation.

Very Canadian.

It will tuck nicely into a collection of short stories between the one about the little Saskatchewan Native girl with the clubfoot and the one about the forbidden love between a Winnipeg Mennonite and a Montreal Jew trapped on an ice flow with their dying pet.

The suffocating marriage is almost as proud a Canadian literary tradition as incest, choking on the shoot-out, or structuring a bildungsroman as an Adlerian transactional analysis.

You will be the next Margaret Laurence Atwood.

Cheers.

D.

P.S. I am very busy right now, writing *Roads and highways in Canadian literature* so can't see myself traveling for a while.

Dear Dave-

Oh, dear, I can see you hate my story. How embarrassing. I have written a new version, so here it is. In this one, there is no family (thus avoiding cliché of suffocating marriage). Instead, the woman is dumped by her lover in a donut shop and decides to go on vacation by herself. She goes to see a waterfall and wishes she could push her lover over, but instead, she returns home, and in a brilliant metaphoric reflection of the real waterfall, loses her mind.

-L.

P.S. I thought we had something special.

Dear Louise:

I like the new version. It has character, conflict, and resolution. Your vacation snapshot images remain perfect. As screamy as my criticism made you, it still got you to finish the fucking story.

-D

P.S. While I did feel our walk on the beach was magical, and I love it that you send me your stories, I think my work on roads and highways has to be a priority right now. University life is really competitive and I think I may be on to something new and important here.

Dear Dave:

Thanks for the encouraging comments, but my heart is broken. Another man I know read the story and suggested he wanted more of a plot. Like what if a man woke up with a severed finger in his pocket?

I think there is definitely a gender barrier here. Perhaps I should write stories about explosions and big guns and robots that come alive,

instead of sensitive ones that explore a woman's feelings.
Offended,
Louise
P.S. Whatever you say.

Dear Louise:

There is compromise between what you have identified as masculine and feminine narrative tendencies. Your second draft showed that.

You do not need laser-guided exploding robot monsters and heaving bosoms to keep men interested in a narrative. It certainly can be easier with such elements, especially the bosoms, but if character, conflict, and resolution are in place you have a good framework to gingerbread up with all the poetic, thematic, self-indulgent literary imagery you need to get you through the night. If you refuse the framework then call it poetry and find another audience.

Just make sure there is a destination at the end of the literary trail. . . preferably one with cold beer and strippers available. Remember. . . masculine readers, not necessarily men, but readers with a need or desire for the patterns and conceits of masculine narrative, will not dig too deeply to decode the inner meaning of your personal symbol set.

Therefore, make sure you at least provide clues to your point. . . and for goodness' sake, have one. Just how many rustic barnyard sunsets and smoggy Toronto mornings do we need enshrined in CanLit? At the standard and oft-quoted image-to-written-word exchange rate we could probably trade in our entire pantheon for a couple of CanLit coffee-table books and a handful of faded postcards and Polaroids and still owe two sonnets and a rude limerick. I find more literary value in vintage Canadian Victory Bond posters than I do in all of Timothy Findley. . . and I like Timothy Findley.
D.

Dear Dave -

How about this for a plot - a small boat on the Amazon, a big snake, a madman, and bosoms?
L.

Louise, that's the plot to the movie *Anaconda*. Why do you want to be a writer anyway, when you have a perfectly good job as a librarian? -D

D.

Maybe you're right but I've always thought that being a writer is like being a lesbian. It's hard to fake it for long, but if you are one, it just doesn't work to live with a man.

The problem I have is, what kinds of stories do we need to write? It seems to me that everything's been written—we've had Chekhov and James Joyce and Mavis Gallant, and Harlan Ellison. Who needs me? My stories all seem to be My Life, which wears pretty thin and pisses off my relatives no end. -L.

Louise -

According to the dictionary, a story is a narrative designed to engage or entertain the reader. As you say, do you really think fictionalizing details of your life will accomplish this? -D

D - oh, you're so helpful. I was hoping somehow to illuminate the human condition.

L.

Louise - The human condition. Who needs the human condition? It's never good news. With all this pressure, what I want is some distraction. -D

Dear Dave -

For distraction, here is my latest story version. The woman, who now has no husband or lover, goes on vacation, meets a robot who pushes her over a waterfall and along the way, her shirt falls off, revealing nice bosoms.

-Louise
P.S. Richard really likes it.

L - Thanks. I like it, too. Can you describe the bosoms a little more?
 -D
P.S. Richard who? By the way, I think I can get away to see you in about two weeks. I will bring my first chapter: *Roads in early 19th century writing of Saskatchewan* and read it to you. It's a bit long-—15,000 words, but I think you'll really love it.
Call you soon,
Dave

Interlude: Creative Spirit Guides

Writing prompt 1

Yesterday at coffee with Lorie, she talked about invoking a creative spirit guide. It sounded exciting, something I would like to try.

My first spirit guides will be knowledgeable experts. At the public library, while searching for something to read, I browsed through the literature section of the Dewey Decimal classification and came across an old friend of my youth—Henry Miller. How had he aged, I wondered. I took the book home, delighted to find an essay called *On Writing*.

Miller said, "Immediately I heard my own voice I became enchanted." Often imitating the writing of his heroes, Miller found himself to be a failure, at rock bottom, a failed writer, a failed man. At that point he found his own voice and launched a successful writing career. As he grew to know and love his own voice, success in the eyes of the world became less and less important. Writing itself was the enchantment and the inspiration. (It must have helped him to be supported by many admiring women.)

Thus inspired, I go to stop number two, the home of a friend who opens her house to a small circle of women who meet once a month for support and writing practice. Once again, it is not the money, the fame, the glory that motivates us, but the elusive enchantment of discovering a singular voice.

Third phase of invocation: Some writing practice. Be careful. You may find that you have taken on another addiction along with your coffee drinking and chocolate loving. You may prefer to write than to scrub the kitchen floor, cook supper or spend time with your husband. This may lead to serious problems: "Yes, I wanted you to write but can't we have some clean laundry, too?"

You may find yourself selective about who you spend time with—only friends who can discuss writing need apply. Only admirers of your words can be allowed to interrupt the flow of words. And at that point there is no problem filling the white pages or computer files. All that you encounter—a friend's tale of woe, a situation in a grocery store, a stray idea, becomes grist for the writing mill.

I am moved by the image in the book I am reading that says journal writing for some people is like taking a little dog on a big leash for a quick shit on the street corner once a day. Just deposit a little pile of crap on these pages. Your holy clean white pages—your holy shit given as a gift to the world.

Footnote: what you don't need to know to be creative: the meanings of words such as 'deconstruction' 'semiotics' or 'textual criticism.'

Writing prompt 2

Still no contact with creative spirit guide. Oh well.

Coca Cola

On Saturday mornings we plunked ourselves down in front of the new television set to be entertained by *Horse Opera*, featuring bad guys in black hats and moustaches, good guys in white hats, stagecoaches with backward spinning wheels, the posse, the sheriff, the rancher and horses with clip-clopping hooves. Eventually guns would be fired. I didn't know what to make of the plot, but we wouldn't miss it. At noon my mother would bring my younger brother and me a hamburger made with buns she had baked herself, as well as one glass of Coca Cola. We were allowed one glass a week of the sweet bubbly drink, which we drank with relish. "Please give us another glass," we would beg, but the answer was always, "NO. Only one glass."

My brother and I had different ways of enjoying our drinks. He would take small sips, spacing them with bites of the hamburger bun, so drink and burger were finished at the same time. I liked to eat the burger, then gulp down the whole Coke at once, a splash of pleasure. Waiting for the drink made it magical, precious.

One Saturday, a disaster. I'd saved my drink as usual, anticipating the moment I could have a full glass and my brother would have none. But when I reached for the small plastic glass, I knocked it over and the whole full container spilled on the floor. I was aghast. My mother heard the crash and raced in with a damp cloth, furiously wiping the Coke. "Why can't you be more careful." She left the room and I waited for her to bring a second serving. Nothing. "Mom," I called tentatively, not sure about the level of her ire. "I need some more."

"No," she called back. "You get one glass. You had it. I can't help if you decide to spill it." I looked at my brother, who tilted his head back to drink his last carefully parcelled drops. NO way was I getting any. "Ah," he said with a happy smile. I sat stunned. A whole week with no Coke. The hamburger stuck in my throat, which tears were about to lubricate.

That spring my second brother was born, a tiny monkey who kept my parents even more distracted and cranky than usual. One Sunday morning my dad took my brother and me to church, leaving my mother and the baby sleeping. After a somnolent service that included both endless English and an infinite German sermon on topics we had no way of understanding, we staggered back into the sunshine where my dad suggested we have lunch at Dairy Queen. Unheard of. Usually lunch was a roast chicken, roast potatoes and canned peas at home, with perhaps some relatives thrown in to add to the tedium. Dairy Queen. Yes, yes! The Dairy Queen Brazier was located about half a block down the road from the church. There we would be given the wonders of a fast food hamburger, not one made by a mother but one in which all the patties would be the same size and shape. An important choice awaited us. Chocolate milkshake or glass of Pepsi? Pepsi was not Coke, but to my undiscriminating cola-loving mind it was just as good. My brother chose the milkshake. I thought for a while and took the Pepsi. Cola was in such short supply, I needed to get it while it was available.

We ate our burgers and shared an order of onion rings, an exotic dish only to be found at DQ or A&W. I gulped down the Pepsi as I ate, having learned from my earlier mistake not to defer pleasure. You never knew what might happen. When I emptied the glass, my dad offered me another one. I was astounded. Did he not follow the Rule of One? Maybe not. Maybe the rule didn't exist independently, but was forged only in the iron will of my mother. I accepted the drink eagerly. What would happen if I did it again? I drank it down, smacking my lips. He offered me another. What parenting planet did he come from? I saw that Dad was different from Mom, and that I must try to pry them apart more often. I drank another one. I finished the burger, finished the onion rings. Drank another. I never had the opportunity to drink as much cola as I could desire. All my dreams were coming true. Next on the menu: vanilla soft ice cream cones.

I didn't have a choice here. At my age we were given the cheapest dessert on the menu. Banana splits were not affordable for families with children. Adults got the splits. Anyway, the bananas were yucky. I ate the ice cream cone, and then we climbed into the car for the ride home. I became aware of an uneasy feeling in my tummy. A queasy feeling, a not nice feeling. I lurched forward. Pepsi poured out of my stomach, nose, mouth. Poured out all over the car, along with a slurry of burger, bun, onion and ice cream. Horrible. A horror of a mess. My dad was beside himself. At home my mother questioned him closely about what he had given me. Four large glasses of Pepsi. What was he thinking? The reason for the one glass limit became clear. It was to prevent us from puking. It wasn't just one of those adult rules we were always running into. It had a purpose. I lay on the couch, empty, my dad glaring at me as he carried pail after pail of water to the car. That was the first time I hit bottom in my junk food addiction.

Rainbow Ice Cream

The preacher glared from the platform that had been rigged for him in the lakeside revival tent. Even at ten in the morning, the sun beat down and we all thought of cool waves. In the stuffy air, my dress stuck to my legs. As if it wasn't bad enough to miss a morning of swimming, I'd had to wear last year's dress that was now slightly too small. The preacher had one of those funny beards that goes under a chin. He wore a dark suit, and drops of sweat rolled down his forehead. He pulled out a large white cloth and dabbed at the drops. Finally, he began. "Except as ye become as one of these"—and he pointed straight at me—"ye shall not enter the kingdom of heaven." I was bewildered. My dad often called us creatures of the darkness and I wasn't sure what the preacher was getting at. "Innocent as the little children, wise as serpents," he continued. I saw his point. My deviousness was well known in our family, the lengths I would go to trick my brother into giving me the last cookie.

My mind drifted to cookies, ice cream, swimming. Suddenly I woke up. "Those will be cast into everlasting darkness. There is a place of gnashing teeth, of fiery torment. Except you receive Christ into your heart, except ye kneel and confess the darkness in your heart, you will be thrown into that torment." I didn't want the torment. I saw my sins. I had a dark heart, everyone said so. I was mean to my brothers, even the baby who was now a toddler. Just the other day, I switched the shoes on his feet. He was still tottery and stumbled along, then fell and started to cry. Remorse filled my heart. I hated myself bitterly for the horrors of my unloving ways. I had no love for anyone or anything except ice cream. The preacher bowed his head. "Lord, fill these people's hearts with remorse and a need for your salvation. Lord, you know who is convicted of sin here. Bring them forward." He raised his head. "We will now sing, *Just as I am,* and anyone who wishes to confess his sins and accept Jesus can come to the front, where helpers will guide you and pray with you."

The crowd began a slow, ragged chorus of *Just as I am, without one plea, but that thy blood was shed for me, and that thou bidst me come to thee. O Lamb of God, I come, I come.* An uncomfortable feeling squeezed my chest. NO, oh no. Not this. Not this need to rise, to have everyone's eyes on me, including the eyes of my dad, who suddenly woke up. *Just as I am, and waiting not to rid my soul of one dark blot, to thee whose blood can cleanse each spot, O Lamb of God, I come, I come.* I am at the front, I have started to cry.

The preacher beckons to a woman who takes me off to the side of the tent where we kneel. She puts her hand on my head, and prays, "Jesus, take this child." She asks my name, and whether I accept Jesus into my heart. I nod, crying. Tears pour down my cheeks along with snot strings. We pray and sing a little. *Just as I am, though tossed about, with many a conflict, many a doubt, fighting and fears within, without, O Lamb of God, I come, I come.* Time goes by. I get up. I am saved.

I look around, but my parents are gone. It is still hot, the sun blazing. I walk along the road to our tent but no one is there. I crawl into it, take off my sweaty dress, put on shorts and a t-shirt. After some thought, I take those clothes off and put on my bathing suit. I head down the dusty road to the beach. My parents aren't there either.

I lie in the sand in the hot sun, wondering how I am supposed to feel as a saved person. Will I stop tormenting my brothers? After a long time, my brother Dave runs across the sand to me. "We had ice cream. I had rainbow. We waited but you didn't come."

My parents trudge along behind Dave, carrying blankets, pails, a diaper bag. "Where is my ice cream?" I call.

My mother says, "It's too hot to carry an ice-cream all this way. It would melt. You can have one another time."

Rage fills my heart. I know that they will forget and I will not be able to enjoy the rainbow flavour I love: blue, purple, pink, all swirled together. I feel hate. I get up and kick sand into my brother's eyes. He screams. My dad grabs my arm, and starts hitting me on the bum. I scream, I writhe and wrestle.

"Go to the tent," my mother shouts. I run away crying. At that moment I realize I have made the wrong choice. Next time I will take the ice cream over the salvation.

Interlude: Recipe and Poem

This section is for my mother, to inspire her to sell lots of copies of my books.

Here is a family recipe that she made when we were children:

Crown Roast of Wieners

Take a pound of wieners, arrange them in a casserole dish in a crown shape, then in the middle, place one diced onion, one can of mushroom soup, and a half a cup of bran. Add one cup of water, then bake in the oven for 45 minutes at 350 degrees. Yum!

This poem is especially for my mother..

Seasons

To you out there:

Come for a secret hour across deep time.
You are blooming like a summer morning.
Feel the sun.
See how red gold leaves fall.
Wander like soft rain,
Dance lightly with love.
Leap these long days and
celebrate this wine sky
and her moon child.

Hear spring evening's balmy wind
whisper strange dreams and
blow colour over cold snow
through earth's chill sleep.

A thousand spirit songs will turn winter green.

Making Baby Nathaniel

School ended early so they took the bus downtown to the Dollar
Giant where they were excited to find bags of cheap candy: Wonka
Sour Nerds, mint green lifesavers and gummibears. Back at his place
they ate the candy and threw the wrappers on the living room floor for
his mother to pick up later. When it was finished they looked at each
other, not sure whether they wanted to play Mario Party 3 or kiss for
awhile.

It was forbidden to be alone in the house kissing. It was playing with
fire.

However, they had a mature relationship that could handle fire. This
wasn't the silly dating of junior high. This was a responsible relationship.
This was high school. They were like adults, except not as ugly.

"I was reading a book, " she said, "and it was about a vampire and he
fell in love with a girl and wanted to make her into a vampire too, and
she loved him and wanted to be a vampire, but in the end they decided
not to, because it was better for her, and I cried. You should read it."

He shrugged, not sure that vampire lovers were what he wanted to
read about. He preferred Shonen Jump – lots of action and very few
words. "Do you want to see my room?"

"Okay, she said, and they ran up the stairs.

Snack Bar Girl

The boss was yelling at me for not making cheeseburgers properly. She said her feet hurt and she was fed up with girls who couldn't figure out the simple process: take the money, put the fries down into the hot oil, throw patties on the grill, open buns onto plates, flip the patties and put cheese or a fried egg on top. Then fill the shake machine with ice cream, pour in chocolate or whatever, turn the machine on, lift the fries out and dump them onto a plate, stick the patties on the buns, add ketchup, mustard, relish, lettuce or tomatoes, close the bun, turn off the shake machine, pour it, and serve it all to the customer. Take the next order: easy-peasy.

Earlier in the evening, I had left the lid off the shake machine, causing ice cream to fly all over the place. Just now I had put the cheese on the patties before they were flipped, turning them into a messy goo to scrape off the grill. These mistakes slowed us down for the backlog of scowling bowlers who wanted their food quickly in between turns.

Mostly I worked by myself in the suburban bowling lanes snack bar except on busy league nights when another girl named Karen came in. She had dropped out of school and lived by herself in an apartment nearby. Her life plan was to make fries and burgers and meet somebody who would be her boyfriend. He would have a job and they could improve their lifestyles together. Sometimes she came in to work with a terrible hangover. If the boss wasn't around, she would sit in the back room and moan while I ran around trying to cook all the food myself.

After scraping the grill, I escaped to the back room where there was a large machine for washing dishes. All during the evening I picked up used plates, stuck them in piles in the back room, and when I had a few minutes, ran back to scrape cold French fries, hamburger crusts, patty crumbs, and other debris into large garbage bins. Then I would stack the plates, glasses and forks into the machine, close the door and turn on the hot water. In fifteen minutes, I would lift the clean hot dishes out and carry them back and stack them onto shelves at the front. They were the thick plates of coffee shops, practically unbreakable and a dirty white colour.

We couldn't leave until all the dishes were done, even if it was later than one in the morning. This dishwashing task was more manageable for me than handling customers and food, but it was hard to admit this to myself after having just graduated from high school with a straight A average.

I got to know some young guys who didn't bowl but came just to hang around. They ate French fries, flirted and made plans to go get drunk later.

Joe was good-looking with blue eyes and curly blond hair but only one arm. He liked to show all the kinds of things he could do with only one arm. A girl came in with a necklace all tangled up and he untied the slender metal thread with his single hand.

Joe liked to look at Karen, but she would bustle by and make me serve him.

"What's wrong with Joe?" I asked her. "You don't seem to like him."

"We used to date but when I broke off with him he killed my dog."

"Killed your dog. What did he do?"

"I found the dog lying by the side of the road, and next time I saw Joe, he kind of smiled at me funny and I knew he'd done it. The dog was named Chow, he was a pug and he was the only person I loved."

I didn't want to mention that a dog wasn't a person, but it seemed odd that she assumed it was Joe.

"What if it wasn't Joe?" I asked her.

"Well, it was kind of strange balling a man with one arm. His dick was okay, though, if you want to go out with him."

I didn't want to go out with Joe, because I was living with Ron.

"It's okay, me and Ron are getting married." We weren't really getting married, I just said that, because I thought you had to marry a person you slept with. Actually, I wasn't even sure I liked Ron any more. He was always mad at me and complained about things I did, how I wore my hair, what I said, all kinds of stuff like that. It seemed that he no longer liked anything about me, and refused to admit it, except to say that he was suffering pressures at school. He wasn't getting the grades he'd been led to expect as the smartest person in his family of five children. He had always been the star but now in university he was just scraping by. He accused his professors of hostility and prejudice toward a person from a poor background. I tried to do my best at work and at home, but sometimes this all got discouraging. I didn't want to break up, though, because I couldn't think of anything better to do if I was alone.

One day as I was pouring coffee, Joe was at the counter and he said to me, "Did you see *Friends* last night?"

"No, I was reading. I don't have a TV."

"Hey, it was funny, you should watch it some time."

We chatted for a bit like that and then he said he had two tickets to a concert Friday night and could I go?

"No, there's my boyfriend," I replied.

"Tell him you're working. I'll meet you in front of the Commodore at nine. It's Mortal Coil."

"Oh, I don't think so," I said. I didn't know Joe very well and didn't think we'd have much in common. Plus there was the whole problem of explaining to Ron how I was going to a concert with another guy. Also, I have to admit that the whole dog thing was a little weird. It didn't sound right, but you never know.

Then Joe started to tell me about the accident, drinking, car crash, fifteen years old and the arm was gone. He got depressed and quit school, left home and his girlfriend broke off with him and now he lived by himself in a crummy room and didn't have any friends and took welfare. So wouldn't I change my mind?

"Okay," I said, overwhelmed by this sadness. "I'll meet you Friday at nine by the front door."

I worried about it all the next day which was Wednesday and decided to cancel the date, but on my Thursday shift he wasn't at the snack bar, and I didn't have his number, and Karen wasn't there so I couldn't ask her. Then I worried about it all day Friday at home, when I was't working and I decided to not go. Except when Ron was home he was angry that the dishes weren't done and we screamed at each other for awhile, then he threw the dishes against the wall and I kicked a box of laundry down the stairs, and finally I told him I was going to work.

I wanted to get out of the house. I waited by the bus stop for half an hour, then I changed at Hastings and Main where scary looking men stood around asking for money for food, then I caught a bus up

Granville to the Commodore. At the Commodore people were milling around and smoking grass and it was dark and I felt lonely. I stood and waited and looked at all the faces, waiting for Joe, a man I didn't know and didn't really want to know except as an escape from a man I did know and wasn't sure I wanted to know. I stood and waited while the time went by and the crowds thinned until finally it was 9:30 and it occurred to me that Joe wasn't coming. I'd been stood up by a one-armed man I didn't even like.

There was nothing to do but catch the bus again and do the whole thing backwards. As we rode along the same streets I felt quite tired, but also relieved in a way that he hadn't been there. A part of me was upset to be stood up, although it solved some problems.

It took about two hours to get home, what with the bad bus schedules, and when I arrived back at the house, my friend who lived with us told me that Ron had gone to the bowling lanes to keep me company and take me home.

It was too late to do anything but go up to bed. I woke up about half an hour later because Ron was sitting on top of me, screaming, "Where were you? Where were you?" I was scared and lied, telling him I was just riding around on the bus because of our fight and he calmed down and asked me for sex. I said I didn't feel like it, I was too tired, and turned over. He picked up a pillow and put it over my face so I couldn't breathe and asked me again and again and again. I struggled to breathe, amazed at his cruelty and terrified he would kill me. Finally I gave in and agreed so he would leave me alone.

On Monday I went back to the bowling lanes. I wasn't sure how I felt about Joe or what I would say to him when I saw him.

As soon as I walked in I could see it was one of those nights that Karen wasn't going to be able to handle. She was pale and didn't say hi or anything, and as soon as I got there, she left the snack bar and sat in the back with her head in her hands.

"How are you?" I asked as soon as I had a chance.

"Oh, terrible," she replied. "Me and Joe got together on Friday and we started drinking and didn't quit until this morning at four."

"You and Joe? I thought you were quit."

"Oh, we were ,but he was so sweet and his life is so sad that when he asked me to go out again I said yes. He told me he'd asked someone that he didn't like all that much to a concert and he wanted to blow it off, so

I spent the evening and the weekend with him."

I stood gaping at her and just then someone came to order fries and a cheeseburger so I went to make the food. The leagues were in and suddenly about two dozen people were standing there all wanting to order and I put a dozen patties down, started the shakes, ran to the freezer to get more fries, noticed the patties were burning and quickly flipped them, threw the fries in the basket and put it down, realized the patties were done but I'd forgotten the cheese on three of them, and then had to throw the lot in the garbage when they started to burn. I went to the back room where Karen was lying with her head in her arms. I told her I needed help but she just said I should fuck off.

Back at the counter, crowds of bowlers were starting to look impatient and more wanted to order.

I looked at them, then turned around, went to the back, took off my apron and hung it on a hook. I didn't punch out on the clock, but picked up my stuff and quietly left by the back door without speaking to anyone.

Nobody was at home and I was glad about that. I found my old suitcase, put my clothes and a few other things into it, started to write a note to Ron telling him I was leaving and then stopped, called a taxi, took it down to the bus depot, caught a bus to my hometown and began a new life.

Interlude: Back to Work

Basement dwelling was meeting most of my basic needs, except for cash. I was given a job at the public library to answer questions.

"How can I make a potato clock for my grandson?"

"How many planets are there, like, you know, this week?"

"My brother says pirates are better than ninjas. Is that *really* true?"

"Can you help me? I live in a basement apartment across from a park where young people drink and break bottles and the landlady has changed her phone number so I can't call her and she sends her boyfriend down to collect my rent and he peeps at me and the lock on the door is broken and I have to leave in five days and next time I am going to get a place in Oak Bay but now I have to sell my furniture and I don't have a computer and when I telephone furniture stores none of them are buying and I have some nice stuff and I had to clean the place up and it wasn't easy with all that filth from the backyard because when I work I can make good money in home support but right now I'm not working though I tried to be a commissionaire once but I didn't like it although I was proud to be accepted into the program my age works against me so I have lived in twenty-five places and been in some tight spots but I always find a solution. "

"Oh."

"Well, thank you so much. You've been very helpful, but I must get going."

It's a living.

DUI

She climbed into my car balancing a box of chicken wings and a drink. She was a big woman, nearly six feet tall and hefty with ragged bleached hair, faded jeans and old denim shirt. A new leather vest with fringes completed the look.

"Hi, I'm Tiffany," she boomed.

I was driving three hundred kilometres in a vast boring forest with a few tiny towns scattered here and there. I took a chance on the woman, who seemed safer and better company than a man.

"Beautiful day." I ventured the most innocuous greeting in the universe.

"Yeah," she said. "Want some?"

She opened the box. The wings smelled good. I decided to live dangerously. I picked up a greasy piece with one hand and drove with the other.

"Whoa, that's spicy," I gasped, and she handed me her drink.

"Have this."

I took a sip and gasped again.

"What is this?"

"Um, diet Coke. With some rum."

Rum. An illegal, open, alcoholic drink in the front seat of my car. Now what? I looked at her. I suddenly saw she was a hard woman and she was a bit drunk and it wasn't even eleven. I didn't know what to do.

I doubt I could have talked her into tossing her drink. I know I couldn't have given her the boot, what with her being much taller, stronger and probably meaner than I was. I had no choice. I had to cross my fingers and ride out the trip. "So, what do you do?" I asked.

"Bodywork."

"Oh."

"Restoring cars, fixing them up."

"But you don't have a car yourself?"

"No," she answered sheepishly. "I'm a DUI."

Drinking and driving.

"So for now hitching is how I get around."

Should I establish rapport by mentioning my parking ticket from Arizona that time?

"Got any kids?" she asked.

"Yes, one who is ten. You?"

"I have a fifteen-year-old boy. But I'm raising him right. See, you have to do things together, let them know you're on their side. My son knows I'm his pal, that he can count on me. Last Friday night we had a little party. His friends. My friends. We made a huge bonfire, drank a few beers, and had a great time. If you drink with them, they won't go off and get into trouble. You can watch and take care."

"Ah."

We sat together, meditating on what good parents we were. My son was a Boy Scout. We did bottle drives together.

"You married?"

"Yes," I said, "You?"

"I was married. Kicked him out. I got a little freaked by the guns. I don't mind guns, but this one time we were in bed and just for fun, he started shooting into the ceiling. He accidentally broke one of my favourite dishes, a really beautiful bowl from Hawaii that had a hula dancer on it. I was pissed off and dragged him out the front door. Told him never to come back. Haven't seen him since. He was fun, though, and a good provider, what with his businesses. He really knew businesses."

I didn't ask. I had the feeling that his businesses was none of my business. But she told me.

"He grew. Good at it. Green thumb. The finest Kootenay Gold that would send you to heaven, throw you a party and call you a cab when you were done. We lived good, but car bodies aren't bad either. I miss him. I just couldn't take the guns."

"No," I sympathized. My husband had the annoying habit of filling the sink with hot, soapy water, putting the dishes in to soak and forgetting about them.

The kilometers clicked by; one tree after another in that beautiful BC way. She finished her chicken and sipped her drink. If this was TV, she would push me out now, steal the car and break for a commercial. But it wasn't TV and Beaverdell rolled into sight.

"Here." She pointed to the hotel, one of the only two builidings on the only block of the one street town. I stopped at the other, pulling up at the single old pump.

"I'll just stop here." I said, trying not to sound too happy while stretching nonchalantly.

"You want to a have drink with me and my friends? We have great times. You could finish your drive later." Far from being a dangerous offender, I saw that she was my friend now, that she was nearly crying at this parting. For a moment I was tempted. Maybe I could have a life that was wilder, lawless. Maybe I could shoot guns into the ceiling.

But the idea of drinking with her crew filled me with terror. Before she could press the invitation, I locked the doors, stepped on the gas, and kicked up a cloud of dust as the car hit the gravel road at the edge of town at speed. The rest of the trip was long, but I didn't mind the boredom any more.

Brothers

1. Karl

Karl hugged his twin brother Dan in the airport lounge, aware again of the two inches and forty pounds he still had on his earlier-born twin. "Hey, bro," he said and they punched each other in the arms before sitting down and quickly downing two Labatt's.

"How was the tour?" asked Karl.

"Oh, man, awful," Dan shook his head. "One night we played Kenora, stayed up late in the motel and I woke up to see freakin' Vince lying on the floor in a bunch of puke. I tried to wake him up, kicked him, but he was down so we had to have him hauled away. Alcohol poisoning. So without a drummer it was no go for the whole rest of the Ontario tour. And that was only the border. So I'm broke and living with the folks."

"Bummer," said Karl. "I'm doing okay in Grande Prairie, sold half a million in only six months."

"Cripes, half a mil" said Dan. "The old man must be proud."

Karl thought—no, knew—that his dad would be overjoyed at the success of his second-born (but by only twenty minutes) son.

He remembered the birth. For months he'd been swimming along fine in this nice dark quiet place, when something kicked him in the head. He tried to avoid the fucker, but as the days went by, the kicks got closer and closer, until it was hard to find any room, or even move. It was always a fist in the eye, or a butt in the face. One day Karl was woken out of a nice peaceful sleep by waves pushing and squeezing him, an intensely uncomfortable feeling. He looked around and saw a sort of tunnel with a faint light at the end, and made for it. The other creature was going there, too, and Karl kicked, punched and clawed to be first, but the other one was suddenly sucked into the black hole, headfirst, and disappeared. Finally there was a little room to move around, and he was just making himself comfortable when the squeezing began again. Terrified, Karl found himself drawn toward the opening, his head thrust down into an impossibly tight space, then his shoulders, his butt, and then he whooshed out into a place that stabbed his eyeballs with light. He was grabbed, then slapped, and he screamed with fear, before he found himself stuck onto something wet, warm and wonderful. He opened his mouth, gulping, and then felt the familiar kicking. Loathing for this being filled his heart and he swore that he would have revenge someday for the creature taking his space.

At the bar, Karl threw down a bright red fifty dollar bill, knowing that with his brother's tour of Ontario bars canceled, Dan would, as usual, not have the cash to ante up. Although Karl had lost the desperate struggle between them to be born first, he now felt it had given him an edge to succeed in life that Dan didn't seem to have. The two brothers laughed and joked as Karl described his job in northern Alberta, an untapped market that the Whole Life Company had given him to test his mettle as a newly promoted life insurance salesman. Karl followed in the footsteps of his father, now a manager with the company, while the slightly older brother still imagined a musician's life.

They were big, tall men of Icelandic origin, blonde, blue-eyed and ruddy-cheeked, full of strength and energy to meet whatever. Karl knew he could down a case of beer and still get up happy to sell life insurance, while Dan scorned the weakness of his drummer who had lain unconscious in pools of vomit in a crummy motel in Kenora. Their clothes reflected different lifestyles: as a man of substance Karl wore a long camel hair coat, a white shirt, dark pants and polished leather shoes; Dan was encased in an old down jacket and pair of frayed jeans.

Boarding, Karl was pissed off to see the small, tightly packed seats of the aircraft, happy that he wasn't sitting beside his brother, but behind him, which meant that they could still joke around, and wouldn't have to compete for arm space.

After awhile a woman sat down beside Karl; a plain, older woman, but he supposed he could step up to the plate of making her a bit happier.

"Hi," she said, looking at him sideways and reaching for her in-flight magazine.

He figured he could do better than the magazine for her. And the opportunity to talk to a middle aged stranger would hone his salesman's skills.

"Hi," he said with enthusiasm, "I'm Karl, your flight mate for the evening."

She smiled and did not return to the magazine. So far so good.

After the plane lifted and the signs went off, Karl flagged the stewardess for two more beers. "Want one?" he asked the woman.

"No thanks, it would put me to sleep."

"Where you from?"

"I'm flying from Victoria to see my mom in Winnipeg. You?"

"I've been working up in Grande Prairie, and we're going to Gimli for a family reunion. I picked up my brother in Calgary – that's him in front."

Dan lifted his hand for a wave and stuck buds in his ears.

"What kind of work do you do?"

"I'm selling for Whole Life, following in my dad's footsteps. He's a manager."

"I'm sorry," she said.

Sorry? He decided she hadn't heard him properly.

She continued, "I used to work for them a long time ago."

Now Karl felt sorry for her. "Why'd you leave?"

"It's a long story. I'm a librarian now."

He thought he wouldn't mention that she was too old to get on with the Company now, if she still wanted to. He took off his glasses and rubbed them on his shirtsleeve. He wondered whether she'd notice how expensive they were, the latest style, square with green frames. He didn't suppose that many guys his age—twenty-three—would be able to pay with company benefits for their own top-of-the-line glasses. His brother didn't wear any, which was good, because it would have been another bone of contention of what Karl had that Dan didn't.

"Your brother work for the company, too?"

"Nah, he's a musician, plays in a bar band. A good guy, though. I guess not many guys my age know what they want to do."

"That's what you wanted to do, work for Whole Life?"

"Well, yeah."

Her face creased up. "You must be Icelandic, going back to Gimli."

"Yes, we are. You?"

"I'm a Mennonite from Winnipeg."

"Hey, they're good. Some of the ones I've met can really hold their own in a bar."

Her face creased again, not in a happy way.

"You ever think about your Viking ancestors?"

Viking ancestors? He hadn't actually thought about them. Was that a come-on line? Another peculiar thing to say. By now he was wondering whether he could politely turn to his iPad, but when her eyes looked down toward the in-flight magazine, he thought, no, this is what makes a good salesman. The ability to go on in spite of the other person.

"Grande Prairie is totally awesome."

"Yeah? I lived there for a couple of years."

"Fantastic," he said, and waved to the stewardess for another beer.

"That's a lot of beer. I try to be a little dehydrated to avoid those tiny airplane bathrooms."

"I'm good" he said, and wondered how to move on from this topic.

"Grande Prairie's great," he continued. "This summer we were golfing until midnight, when it's still light. There's this hole, I took a swing, and man, did I hit that thing, right over the trees into the next green, nearly got it in. I love it."

"Have you met people?"

"Mostly people I work with." This was a bit of a sore point. He hadn't really met anyone to speak of, anyone young that is. A woman for example. He only seemed to meet older women. "The girls, I have to beat them off with a stick."

"Oh, you into that?"

Now what? It was a fine line with older women, to charm them into buying the product, but not to charm them too much. Karl had learned that the hard way. He took a plunge in a new direction.

"I'm into the company, you know? It's such a wonderful feeling to sell insurance and then be able to provide for a family in hard times." He allowed his eyes to tear up a little. The woman was looking at him. She didn't say anything.

He decided to bail on conversation. "Hey, you want to watch a show? I have my laptop."

"Uh, sure," she said, and he pulled out the computer and booted up *Californication*. Oops.

She looked for awhile, then closed her eyes and settled back in her seat. He watched the show until the landing announcement came on.

"So what do you think you'll do in Winnipeg?" he asked.

"Maybe go to the zoo."

"I love the zoo. Those polar bears."

"You want to go?" she said.

He felt stunned. An invitation. "Um, no, no, I won't be able to fit it in. Sorry."

Now she looked surprised. "You'll be in Gimli. I just meant, whether you would have wanted to go."

He felt relief. A quick recovery on her part. He let it go. The plane landed, the doors opened, and then it was that rush time when everyone stood up, grabbed their bags and waited in a hot crowd for too long.

"Well, looks like it's time to get off. You have a good visit," he said, but didn't add, 'maybe we'll run into each other' with a meaningful look. He didn't trust her to understand that the favour he was suggesting to her wasn't serious.

"Yes, and have a nice life with Whole Life." And she smiled.

"Hey, Bro, another beer?" The brothers stepped off, laughing and ready for a good time.

2. Dan

As Dan waited for his brother in the airport lunge he thought about the Ontario tour that had fallen apart right at the beginning because of his drummer's stupid drinking. The tour was supposed to be the turning point, four months of gigs across the Province that his manager had scored when another band had fallen through. After the Kenora incident, Scottie told Dan never to show his face again as long as he lived, which wouldn't be long probably. Dan chuckled to think of it now. And then he'd gone on to Calgary to play bass for a friend who owed him. Why couldn't the guy have come up with another drummer?

It was a good time to regroup his forces and go back home to the folks for awhile. They were getting on, in their fifties now, and could use some help cutting lawns and so on. They didn't mind, anyhow, now that Karl was safely stowed in Northern Alberta, apparently being a genius life insurance salesman. Poor idiot. Dan hoped that his pity wouldn't show through, pity for his brother's strange desire to work hard at the insurance business. He supposed it came from being not his mother's favourite all during their growing up.

After Dan had made the finish line first, his mother had taken one look at his curly blonde hair and had fallen in love with him. The second brother coming shortly afterward didn't rate much of a look, although his mother did feed them both with her ample and flowing breasts that Dan didn't like to think about now, but which had obsessed him every minute for months in his early life.

And there he was, coming through the gate all dressed to the nines and smiling. "Hey, bro, looking good, looking good." Dan exclaimed and hugged his brother, aware of the forty pounds his brother had on him, another sign of too many big lunches in the business.

They sat for awhile, knocking back the brew and catching up. Then it was time to head for security again, board and sit down. Karl's seat mate was pretty and looked interesting, but Dan knew to leave her alone, as his charm had taken many a wench from his brother, who had never known what to say to the chicks. Dan merely waved his hand and settled down to music. He could vaguely hear them laughing and chattering behind him and he hoped that the woman could put up with his brother's dull conversation that invariably led to how much he loved insurance. Dan hoped to make music his whole life. It wasn't a rich lifestyle, but he knew that in the end, the hard work and never giving up would pay off. In the meantime, he enjoyed himself and made his parents laugh and his friends happy. He tried not to rub it in that Karl had drawn the short straw all around.

Interlude: The Worst Comedy Set Ever

I was facing a crowd with an average age of eighty-five. I'd been asked to do a stand-up comedy set at a seniors' retirement home by my comedy teacher Kirsten. Although I hadn't wanted to tell jokes to old people, Kirsten had access to jobs that paid and if I did her a favour, she might hire me for something. I was living in my brother's basement rent-free, but this gave him an upper hand in unsettling ways. Not directly stated ways, but in the dynamics of our family, my occupying his basement without charge meant that he had won the game of life and could now feel superior to me and could ask me for favours, such as taking his laundry to the dry cleaners or making him spaghetti. After asking for favours, he might say, "I don't want you to feel useless."

I wasn't useless. I was writing a novel. I was performing stand-up comedy. I was working on my inner life. Just because these endeavors weren't currently paying well didn't reflect on my value in this world. Some day it would all pay off, but in the meantime, I was attempting to get into the good graces of comedy diva Kirsten. I was annoyed when she phoned to cancel her own participation at the last moment. "I sent a sub," she said airily. "I'm sure you'll all do great." I knew this sub, a glowering hulk of a comedian who never smiled unless the right people were laughing at his jokes. People with money.

So now it was my turn at the microphone. I stepped forward confidently. Okay, I was pretending confidence. The first four comics hadn't raised a laugh. The oldsters couldn't hear them, or understand their references. I felt they wished we were Bob Hope, or Phyllis Diller, or anybody but who we were: amateurs with a limited range.

Hello. How are you? Still alive I see. Well, enjoy, it's not going to last much longer. I'm older, too, and I'm writing a sequel to the acclaimed novel *Fifty Shades of Grey*, called *Fifty Shades of Grey Hair*. You might like it. It is full of tips for older folks, like using Velcro instead of ropes in your BDSM fun and games. You know how urgently we need to go to the bathroom sometimes.

Have any of you ever seen an ad like this: "Eighty-five percent of women are wearing the wrong bra size." Then you go and get fitted and the ads promise you will look absolutely gorgeous. Well, women will do anything to be better looking. So I see the ad, and think 'Yeah, right. . . .' but I'll try anything, so I went in, and the saleslady said, 'Honey, What's your bra size?' I told her, but I won't tell you, and she said,' Oh, you're wearing the wrong size bra.' I'm thinking, no way, I'm in my thirties, this isn't rocket science. I'm good.

So she brings this thing and I try it on and I tell you, *Zero Dark Thirty* waterboarding has nothing on putting this on (act out). 'No, I think it's wrong,' I say.

'Well, you look marvelous.' she tells me.

She's lying, I know it. There's no way I could look marvelous no matter what size bra I wear. And it hits me, this woman's going to be staring at my breasts for the next hour if I don't get out of here now. And I'll be dropping a hundred bucks. She looks at me and I can read her mind: 'How much money can I get out of this poor bitch???'

It's not a bra they're selling, it's self delusion. . . .

Whew. I went back to Zeller's, which was still open then, and purchased my usual 'Fifty Shades of Beige One size fits women with low self esteem' for ten bucks.

Thank you, you've been a wonderful audience.

Nobody laughed.

Artist in the Country

The car jolted through clouds of dust and endless fields of waist-high green grasses. Barley? Wheat? Who knew. How long would they have to drive on this unpleasant gravel road? After an hour Sue and Tom stopped by the side of the road to take a break. Heat pressed down on them from an immense sky, dead quiet except for the insect hum. Sweat crawled down Sue's back like insects. Maybe it was insects. Tom smoked a cigarette beside the car. "Not much farther to go," he told Sue. Henry St. Clair, the artist and Tom's mentor, lived in the middle of nowhere.

"How can he stand it out here?" she asked.

"His property has trees and a creek running through it," replied Tom. "I was there once. If you don't like it now, you should try the middle of winter. The time I came it was February, forty below and their furnace wasn't working too well. The windows were covered with ice on the inside. We drank all night and talked about painting. It was a fine time. Henry's a great old guy. You'll like him." Tom finished smoking and they got back into the car.

The heat glued Sue's legs to the vinyl seats. She shuddered.

Henry St. Clair slashed at a large canvas with broad, excited red and yellow strokes. He was close. He could See. It was coming together at last. He turned for more red. He turned back in time to catch the enormous work in his arms as five-year-old Sam took up a defensive position behind the toppled easel. Bang. Bang. His little sister covered him from the door. Henry looked from the spoiled canvas to his laughing children with horror and disbelief. He bared his teeth and screamed, "Catherine."

Sam retreated. He grabbed little Annie's arm, and still laughing and squealing, they made for the creek and all its magical hiding places.

Catherine was lying down. It was just for a minute, but her eyes had closed and she had drifted off to a large table covered with tasty dishes she didn't have to cook. She started awake, her husband's rage in her ears. No. The children knew that they must not, absolutely must not, disturb Henry in his studio. He needed to paint. He needed to sell. They needed a new roof. June rain had poured into the living room. It warped the floor and ruined the Afghan carpet. So much money. Henry had to paint.

She struggled out of bed and made her way down the creaky stairs, across the yard to the barn, "What's wrong?"

"Those kids. Look at the painting. It's wrecked. Bits of straw stuck to the wet paint that had smeared off the canvas and on to Henry and the floor. "Can't you watch them for one minute? That Sam is a devil. You should have seen him with his guns, wanting to kill me. Full of hate."

"Oh, it's not hate." replied Catherine wearily. "He wants to have some fun. It's so boring out here in the country, no TV, no friends. He's just little."

"And he's your job. He's all you do. You only have to do one thing, which is to keep those kids away from me and you can't even do that. God knows you won't cook."

Catherine turned and stomped off. This was not the retreat to the country she had imagined. When they had talked it had been pastoral, natural, and romantic. The reality was primitive, bleak and isolated. Rodents. Bugs. Stinks. And she had imagined twenty-first century plumbing, not the ad hoc nightmare of pumps and pipes that never really worked.

She remembered Henry at the beginning, when they'd met at one of his shows. She held a drink and a canape and smiled at him. That was all it took. He pursued her relentlessly, even though he had been married to the beautiful Angela, thin, dark, intense Angela. She had believed in him. She had promoted him. She had made Henry. She gave him everything he wanted. And then Henry wanted Catherine. The affair had nearly destroyed all three of them. It drove Henry and Catherine to their country retreat, where Sam was quickly followed by Annie.

She stared out towards the road and saw the plume of dust and remembered Henry's friends. She thought she'd better clean something or cook something. Were these people actually thinking of staying the night? She wasn't sure the septic field was up to another two people. Where were the kids?

Henry stood by the splotched painting. His magnificent vision was lost.

He was surrounded by plagues: his ex-wife was ever more successful promoting other artists; his new agent was pressing him for work for another show, even though he had not sold anything at the last one. Catherine was always crying. His children were powerful and unmanageable.

Catherine had been so beautiful, the blond goddess at his Spring Trees opening. He had never been so captivated by blondness, by pale translucent skin, by youth, by large luminous blue eyes. It wasn't that he hadn't loved Angela. They were together for twenty years, clawing a life out of fine art. He'd just been unable to resist Catherine's eyes, her smile. Her body had inspired him to create, to live, to paint, to feel. Together they made love, laughter, tears—life. It was too much for Angela. She demanded that Henry make a choice.

Henry didn't understand. Surely she could understand the demands of passion? She threw him out and destroyed his paintings of a naked Catherine. He found the fragments in a bin in the alley. He went to Catherine. She took him in. She was luminous and adoring and beautiful and Henry sloughed off middle age like a skin, leaving him new and young and ready for more love, more freedom and more sex.

He set the ruined painting back on the easel and wiped off his brushes. Tom and, the girl, (Sue, was it this time? It was always a different girl) would be there soon. The idea of a third wife crossed Henry's mind. Maybe the answer to his current dilemma of a crumbling country house, the discontent all around him, was a third wife with a good job. She would have no children or desire for them. She could be older. Sensible. She could guide him into his old age and take care of him. He imagined a cultivated life with intelligent adults who would drink martinis in a well-cared for home and discuss art. He could leave Catherine in the country with Sam and Annie. They would understand his need to be in the City, where his career would be reactivated. This new wife would have nothing to do with art. She would have to be something like a financial planner.

A car turned into the driveway. Henry gave them a wave from the barn, admiring Sue's long, thin, tanned body unfolding from their little car. Tom's success had now outstripped his own. Henry suppressed a feeling of annoyance at this. Sure, he enjoyed Tom's undying gratitude, but it didn't fix the roof.

Sue was quiet but lovely. Henry was delighted to learn that she worked as an account manager for Whole Life in the city. During dinner, delayed because Catherine had forgotten to turn on the oven, he called the green-eyed Sue 'my dear' and tried to engage her interest with tales of his early struggles in Montreal.

Sue had trouble concentrating through the noise of the children, who were wild and rude and involved in a running gun battle. Catherine didn't seem to have an inkling of how to make them behave, but sat in the corner drinking wine. Sue thought with some nastiness that Catherine had probably always got by on her looks, and was now in over her head with children and this horrible farmhouse. Why on earth had they purchased such a ruin? Whole Life wouldn't have insured it. Surely Henry was rich enough by now to have bought a nicer place?

It got late and they got drunk. It was clear that Sue and Tom would have to spend the night. Sue's irritation and boredom were overwhelming, but it simply wouldn't be possible to navigate the unmarked country roads in the dark.

"Catherine, is there any more of that delicious chocolate cheesecake?" Henry smiled. Dessert had been a bag of Oreos thrown down at their guests. She looked in despair at Tom, then looked again in surprise. Tom was gazing at her. He was gazing like men had gazed at her in the city. She pushed her breasts out a little more toward him and smiled. Tom smiled back.

"Catherine," said Tom, "Thank you for supper. May I help you with the clean-up? There must be a lot of dishes."

Catherine nodded, smiled and sailed magnificently toward the kitchen, followed by Tom with an armload of plates. There was a pause as Henry looked at Sue. "My dear," he said, "Would you like to see my studio?"

Sue supposed it was unavoidable. They left the house, and walked toward the grey building across the yard. She looked up. Overhead the sky was black and covered with stars, like spilled jewels on velvet. She gasped. It was incredible. She'd never seen so many stars; too much light pollution in the city. A dazzling sky radiated over her head. She couldn't look away.

Henry watched her. Oh, he thought, yes, the stars. Very nice. She must have a romantic nature. "If you'll just come with me into my studio you'll see something really beautiful." He was thinking of his decades of artistic achievement, his new canvases stacked against the walls, representing the fruits of his passionate life and dedication to art, symbols of sacrifice, new work torn out of his living flesh as a gift to the world.

Sue reluctantly left the stars and followed him into the studio barn. In the dim light she saw canvases covered with strokes of colour—red, orange, yellow stabs and blobs. Was this modern art? What could she say? "How wonderful. You must be so proud. But how wonderful for you to see these stars every night. What an inspiration they must be." She wanted to go back outside and stare at the sky full of diamonds again.

They looked at each other. Henry saw that she was unmoved by the beauty in front of her, the beauty he had created. He looked around and saw as she did: grey splintering walls, streaks of paint on squares of canvas, a dirty floor, cobwebs. Then he looked into her green eyes. They were empty, obviously devoid of interest in him or his work. He thought of Angela. She was always so interested. She was nowhere near this place.

Sam and Annie had fallen asleep on the couch after a Mexican standoff. In the kitchen, Tom did the dishes and made Catherine laugh while she rested her eyes and sipped the tea Tom had made.

Spare Change

"Spare some change?"

The thin and tired-looking young guy begging in the early morning light smiled at Lou. She wondered whether he had slept on the hard pavement, or had walked the night away. "Here," she said, and stuck her half-eaten Danish into his outstretched hand. "Hungry, aren't you?" He looked down in surprise, turned away, and threw it into the street.

"Dickhead," she muttered to herself. Wasn't it bad enough to be rehabilitated by working in a crummy shop, without putting up with panhandlers and losers, too? She had no patience with men wanting handouts now that she herself worked for a living. She wondered why they thought she had anything to give, dressed as she was in thrift store castoffs: a red terry-towel bathrobe tied over green tights and pink dance slippers on her feet. The whole outfit had cost less than five dollars. While the outfit flattered the Bohemian look that she had cultivated for the past four decades, it did not speak of money to give away.

She unlocked the door to the charity store where she had been taken on after her fibromyalgia wore out as a reason for welfare, or Benefit as it was now called. When offered the job she had smiled sweetly and pretended to be grateful. She'd learned the cost of angry words to those with power over her funds. The time she'd walked out on her bitchy social worker had led to the whole present fiasco. The Benefit had been small but steady, and now she needed to earn slightly more than minimum wage to cover her rent, groceries, and the occasional treat. This morning she had six quarters in her pocket to cover expenses until the end of the week. Perhaps buying fifty dollar tickets for the Folkmania concert had been a poor choice, but she had to have some fun, didn't she?

Living on what was supposed to be an exciting edge was getting more boring all the time: no money, no work, temporary relationships flaring up before leading to tedious breakups. When she was young she'd prided herself on being unconventional and full of possibilities, but after all these years, she saw that the potential in her mind had never come to what she felt she deserved and that never giving an inch to society's demands maybe hadn't been the best strategy. Well, at least she had kept her figure, not running to fat like some of her friends, but thin and spare, still able to count her ribs in the bath.

The shop, in the middle of a row of shops with dusty windows and castoffs of the sort that seemed to live forever in windows like these, was full of old, smelly donated clothes. Everything on display was so remote from use or desire that it was impossible to imagine a transaction of even a few cents to retrieve them and take them away.

Her job involved hanging up deliveries of donations sent from head office, and selling clothes to customers while balancing cash and making sure the building was in order- easy. She had wanted a more important position—management—but had to start here, at the bottom.

When cut off the Benefit, she'd considered developing insanity as a way to maintain her income, but the effort of appearing crazy was too much for her and so she'd agreed to become a fully functioning member of the work force. Show up on time, with a good attitude, and you will go far, they told her. Well, here she was.

The day moved slowly. A box arrived and she hung the t-shirts, dresses, and pants on the racks. Done with that, she read an old Glamour magazine instead of cleaning the dusty shelves.

In mid-afternoon, a tired-looking woman with three drooly, snotty children and a stroller hung with lumpy bags spent about an hour browsing. At last the woman dumped an armload onto the counter.

"How much?" she asked.

Lou checked the small clothes for price tags: "Seven-fifty."

"I'll give you three bucks for the lot," she said, and stared at Lou.

Lou had been instructed never to give discounts. The charity operated on a small margin and the prices were already low enough for poor people. If she was caught changing prices, she would be fired, and then what? She would have to live on the streets. But she remembered the days when she had two small children, no job, no husband, and resentment toward those who had more. She deserved more, but they had it. How did some people have so much and she so little?

"Okay, " said Lou. What the hell? The woman had a belligerent look in her eyes, three children to deal with, and might be a problem. If she came in here again, asking another staff member for a discount, Lou could deny breaking the rules. In this neighbourhood the customer was always wrong. Up until now Lou had enjoyed taking a hard line with the scam artists who had tried to discount these items, but this time she gave in.

The woman slammed down some coins, grabbed the clothes and stuffed them into bags. "Let's go," she snarled to her kids, who had watched the whole transaction with round brown eyes. Lou smiled at them, pretending to like them as she had been trained in a customer service class, but grateful that her own children were long gone.

She'd tried to stay on welfare by explaining about her single mother status, but her youngest being nineteen meant she didn't qualify. In fact, she didn't even know where the two of them had got to. Her son, she hadn't seen since the winter, when she refused to give him money to buy a guitar. Her oldest, a daughter, at twenty-five, hadn't been around for nearly ten years. Well, they were ungrateful or a pain in the ass. Lou thought about her children as she flipped through the magazine with pictures of styles from five years ago that were actually now in the shop, and then watched the sun slowly change position in its slant through grimy window panes.

At a quarter to five Lou decided to close up and go home. She wanted to leave early to maybe share a pizza with her friend Wayne, who lived in the apartment across the hall. She'd just put the key in the shop lock when a small girl came up to the door.

"Missus, missus, I got these clothes." She held out a greyish pillowcase stuffed full of things that would no doubt smell bad and would have to be tossed.

"I'm leaving." said Lou. "You're too late." She turned to go.

"Please, missus, my mom will kill me if I don't come home with the money."

Money. For this crap.

"We don't give money," Lou snapped, but turned and opened the door for the dirty, shoeless, snaggle-haired child.

"Thank you missus. " she smiled, a light of relief in her dark eyes.

Kids, thought Lou. They're still full of hope and think that things will work out, when actually the world will fuck them over and they don't stand a chance. Lou stomped over to the counter.

"Let's see what you got." She took the bag and dumped it out. As she suspected, a pile of grey and smelly sweaters and blouses, probably being sold by a desperate mother to get drugs.

"This is crap," said Lou.

"Please give me a dollar." The girl stretched her mouth to reveal gap teeth, attempting to charm Lou, succeeding only in looking more desperate. They didn't give money, but Lou thought, poor kid, probably death if she doesn't bring something home. She gave her a dollar from the till and said, "Now get out and don't come again. Tell your mum we don't buy clothes."

When the child had left, she threw the lot in the garbage.

But something bright and glittery caught her eye. She fished around and found a pin in the shape of a Christmas tree on one of the sweaters—a cheap gold pin decorated with bits of coloured glass. She unfastened it and held it in her hand. Then she stuck it in her pocket and locked the door.

She walked three blocks to the dry cleaning shop where she and Wayne lived across from each other in small apartments at the top of a long narrow flight of wooden stairs. Wayne worked as a waiter in a high-class steak restaurant nearby and watched television the rest of the time. He was thin like her, with long grey hair, very tall, always folded into his chair, knees up to support a tray. Other than some occasional semi-drunken sex, they hadn't had a romantic relationship, both suspecting they were too old for the intensity of what they used to consider love, and better off with an easy friendship. Lou glanced around his apartment at the beer case coffee table, the IKEA shelving unit, a pair of black socks lying in front of the large television set among scattered DVDs—two complete seasons of *Oz*, *The Wire*, *Weeds*, and strangely, *Mary Poppins*. His place was a little disorganized but nothing compared with the chaos of her own scattered clothes, empty pizza boxes and burnt-out candles in wine bottles.

"I'm giving up drinking." he said, picking up a beer.

"What's that then?"

"Beer isn't drinking. It's a beverage. Drinking is scotch or rye or gin or tequila."

"I can't afford the pizza," she said, "I blew the grocery money on a concert."

"Not to worry, I've got leftovers from the restaurant—steak, mashed potatoes, and some green beans. We can share."

They ate quickly, watching a *Survivor* episode about a group of people stranded in the outback of Australia.

"Huh. They've got it easy," said Lou. "Try living here on ten bucks an hour. Hey, I've got dessert."

She reached into her pocket for the thin marijuana cigarette that she thought was crumpled at the bottom. "Ouch." she said, as the pin in her pocket pricked her finger.

"What's that?"

"It's this pin."

"Pretty."

"Pretty and cheap," she replied. "I had one just like it when I was a kid. It was Christmas. My dad was alive then. Maybe his last Christmas. I dunno. He had a crummy factory job, a nothing job, but he could do it. He had no education. Anyway, the one good thing was that at Christmas his company threw a party. We thought it was magic. The party was in a big hotel, there was a big tree and a roast beef dinner. See, we had no money and five kids and we never went anywhere, so the yearly do was a big deal. We wore good clothes. I remember white lace stockings and a velvet dress and a hair bow. My mom saved up so my brothers had shiny shoes and she had stiff curled hair from getting it done. My dad wore a suit. We all went down there and felt important and had the meal and then a Santa came and gave us presents. He called our names, we went up there, and got gifts. They were crappy, but the Christmas I was twelve, I got a little gold box and when I opened it, I couldn't believe my eyes—this Christmas tree pin was inside and I thought it was the most beautiful thing I'd ever seen."

"What happened?" asked Wayne, handing it back.

"My dad was sick and then he died and us kids were given around to relatives and foster homes and I guess it got lost. Now here it is again all these years later."

They finished their dinner and wrapped up the evening with a brief hug.

Lou held the pin, placed it on her pillow and fell asleep quickly. She woke up while it was still dark and remembered how it was when her dad was sick. She had gone down to the Catholic church with her most valuable possession, the Christmas pin, laid it before the Virgin Mary and begged for her father's life. She believed that Mary would save him if she made this sacrifice. A few days later her brother met her coming home from school and said that their dad had been taken away in an ambulance and died.

Later, she went back to the church to find the pin, but it was gone.

As she lay in the dark remembering, a terrible pain stabbed her heart. She got up and opened Wayne's apartment door with a key that was hidden under the mat. Moving quietly in the dark, sniffling and moaning, she crept into his room and climbed under the covers, grabbed him and started whimpering into his back.

"Lou, what the . . ?" he turned, startled and groggy.

"I was thinking of my dad. Can I stay here for awhile?"

"Okay, I'm getting a bit damp, though."

They lay together, Lou clutching at his long hair for comfort. "I love you," she said.

"Oh, Lou, I love you too," and he turned to hug her. "You don't want to get married, do you?"

"No, but it's nice that you're here. It's just so awful to think of my dad."

"It'll all be better in the morning. You want a cup of tea?"

"I guess."

They got up, boiled some water and sat at the table in silence. Lou stopped crying. Wayne lit a cigarette.

They watched the sky turn from black to grey to white. Another day.

"I think I can probably stop drinking," said Wayne.

"Maybe after awhile I can find a better job," said Lou. "Do you want to go get some breakfast? At this time of morning there are some interesting people in the donut place."

They dressed, and walked two blocks. Wayne held out his hand to Lou, and she grasped it as they walked. The same cracked pavement greeted them; the same weeds sprang up in the pavement. At the corner, a bundle of newspapers lying on the sidewalk shifted and scattered as the same sad panhandler rose up and asked Lou for money. She turned and looked into his face. His face with the sun behind it was in darkness, but light around his hair dazzled her eyes.

Digging into her pocket, she pulled out a quarter and gave it to him. "Get yourself something to eat," she said, and he blessed her with a radiant smile.

Interlude: Letter to the City

Dear City Works Manager:

As if it isn't bad enough I have to go live in my brother's basement, I now see that the City is working on sewer pipes starting at eight a.m.

I need my sleep. Sometimes I'm up all night working on my novel.

At night I notice that the basement is alive. Mice, mould, frost, disintegration. It breathes as it stoically upholds the house.

I should have been successful. I should have been happy and prosperous. I should have been doing more with my life, a writer with books, awards, true love, gorgeousness, fame, money, riches, lots and lots of wealth.

Instead, alone I go out to the lake to paddle along the lake edge, eat a cheese sandwich, nap on the sand, admire my legs under the murky water, wonder about the possibility of bears, yawn, paddle home, read a paperback mystery, stare at the stars.

It could have been worse. What if I was in the back seat of a taxi with Willie Pickton? We meet at a dance, he's friendly and fun, he's taking me to a party, we're high, he has a place in the country. Game over.

I often think of my mother. She was a young mother with not much money and three children to feed with limited resources. When money was tight we had fried Klik, macaroni with wieners, or a soup made with potatoes, butter and noodles. On Sundays she provided a roast chicken with boiled potatoes and canned peas. Desserts were the main focus of her attention: apple pies, chocolate chip cookies, jellyrolls, brownies, chiffon cake—always something after every dinner, even if only canned fruit or Jello. In the early 1970s homemakers became more prosperous and food become exotic: Chinese beef was the first experiment, including pieces of beef with vegetables like green peppers. It's hard to think back and realize that for those cooks, oregano was new and daring. We all longed for the ultimate treat: ice cream with a chocolate swirl in it—not home-made but store boughten, as we called it.

Where was I? Oh yes, the construction on our street. The afternoon would be a better time for noise. I am often out with friends. I have been meeting X for drinks. Beautiful, young, brilliant, self destructive. A person is not a handful of dust, but a shoebox full of dust. Knowing this makes it even more imperative to feel ourselves as flesh, eyes, mouths, ideas, sensations, emotions, hair, toes, skin, appetites, needs and wants. We meet and talk. The need to flower burns in me. I want to be beautiful and adored. Drunk, we are not beautiful and adored but silly and red-faced. Eventually we fall down or throw up. I saw a shooting star the other day, that flashed by in a sky full of stars. It seemed like a promise, but was really only a burnt out rock. Should we ever hope for anything?

In any case, I hope you will consider my request to start construction later in the day.

Sincerely,
Louise

Coming Home

The last good thing that happened to me was that I went back home to attend my grandmother's funeral, where I was met with strong religion. Everyone was saying, "Hallelujah, she is dining at this moment with her dead children and all her dead friends and dead relatives and they're having a better party than we are, so let's celebrate."

There was her body, lying so still, and my cousins were patting her hands and feeling her face and throwing themselves on her coffin, saying, "Praise be, praise be," and once again I felt like a child in the capable hands of adults who knew the way.

We all remembered and talked about her chicken soup, her saintly patience, and her being secretary of the church women's group for twenty-three years. We all knew that she had been a good woman who did good deeds, unlike her sister, who had also been a good woman, but who had been instructed by God to poison her husband.

During the funeral there were readings, there was testifying, there was praying and singing and a rousing message from my preacher cousin. Afterwards we drove to the cemetery where my grandmother was placed in a peaceful spot full of Thiessens and Friesens so heaven wouldn't feel too different from the North Kildonan Mennonite Brethren Church. We threw flowers on her grave and then went for cold cuts prepared by cheerful church women. There I spoke to my long-lost favourite cousin, and lo and behold, I learned that young Hans Huebert had been called to witness to lost souls in Rosedale, the richest part of rich Toronto. He told me, "Hedge fund managers also need salvation."

And my mother was truly bereaved. She sat at the table, tears falling into her water glass, and we all came and gave her a hug.

Then we went back to my aunt's place where my second cousin talked for about four hours about the good choices he had made since the time twenty years ago when he had been picked up by the police with a marijuana joint in his pocket. Although he didn't refer to the incident out loud, I remembered, just as he probably remembered other unspeakable things about me.

And while he spoke, there sat his lovely silent wife, always smiling. And his three pretty teenage daughters also sat smiling and not speaking. They attended the Mennonite High School and all afternoon they never spoke out of turn but sat nicely on the sofa, listening and learning how to live from their elders.

And then my cousin told a terrible story about one of my classmates, as good a girl as you could hope to be, who, in her naiveté, had married a madman, but from the church, and who now lived in fear for her life.

And I, the wickedest girl to graduate from the Mennonite High School, was living serenely and untouched by any tragedy, and everyone looked at me, and perhaps they were thinking, God's ways are mysterious.

After a while we all went home and I knew then who I was and where I came from and who loved me and what I had to do to keep on being loved.

About the Author

Joy Huebert is an award-winning writer who lives in Victoria, British Columbia. She has published stories and poems in a variety of literary magazines, including *Descant, Grain, Other Voices, Canadian Stories, Island Writer, Horsefly* and *Rhubarb;* the e-zine *Feathertale*, and in three chapbooks from the Root Cellar Press of the Columbia River Writers' Publishing Co-operative. She edited and contributed to Quadra Books' collection of poetry and short stories, *Pathways Not Posted.*

www.ingramcontent.com/pod-product-compliance
Lightning Source LLC
Chambersburg PA
CBHW072046170626
46811CB00008B/3177